Buster and the Dance Contest

by Marc Brown

 LITTLE, BROWN AND COMPANY
New York ·⁊· Boston

Little, Brown and Company, Time Warner Book Group
1271 Avenue of the Americas, New York, NY 10020 • www.lb-kids.com
First Edition
Library of Congress Cataloging-in-Publication Data
Brown, Marc Tolon.
Buster and the dance contest / Marc Brown.—1st ed.   p. cm.   (Postcards from Buster)
Summary: Buster sends postcards to his friends back home when he and his father visit an international
food festival in Wisconsin, where he meets six girls who will be performing a traditional Hmong dance.
ISBN 0-316-15889-5 (hc)/ISBN 0-316-00118-X (pb)
1. Hmong Americans—Juvenile fiction. [1. Hmong Americans—Fiction. 2. Dance—Fiction. 3. Rabbits—
Fiction. 4. Postcards—Fiction. 5. Wisconsin—Fiction.] I.
Title. II. Series: Brown, Marc Tolon. Postcards from Buster. PZ7.B81618Bj 2005 [E]—dc22   2004016168
Printed in the United States of America • 10 9 8 7 6 5 4 3 2 1

All photos from *Postcards from Buster* courtesy of WGBH Boston, and Cinar Productions, Inc., in association with Marc
Brown Studios.

Do you know what these words MEAN?

contest: a game, race, or competition th: people try to win

festival: a celebration or holiday, often with special foods and activities.

lane: a narrow road

perform: to sing, act, dance, or do something else in front of others

rehearse: to practice for a performance

reverse: a change of direction going the opposite way

tournament: a series of contests betwee two or more people or teams

traditional: following customs that have been passed from one group of people to another

Madison, WI

- Madison is the capital of Wisconsin. There is a large group of Hmong people living in Madison.

- Hmong is the name for a group of people from a country call Laos, which is in Asia. Many Hmong have come to the U.S. to live.

- The state animal of Wisconsin is the badger.

Buster put the last thing
into his suitcase.

"Did you forget anything?"
Arthur asked.

"I'm not sure,"
said Buster.

"I won't know till
I get there."

"Wow!" said Buster,
looking around at a giant food festiva

"I feel like I'm in Southeast Asia."

"This is Wisconsin, Buster,"
his father reminded him.

"Well, it tastes like Asia," said Buster.

ASIAN FOODS

House of Wisconsin Cheese

Dear Binky,

Wisconsin produces more than *two billion* pounds of cheese a year.

I wonder how many cheeseburgers you could make with that.

Buster

Dear Arthur,

Wisconsin is famous for cheese.

But I have been eating some great sausages here.

My dad says I'm starting to look like a sausage myself.

Buster

thur Read

O Main Street

lwood City

Buster met the Vang girls
at the festival.

There was Caitlyn, Diane, Tiffany,
Rose, Jocelyn, and Amanda.

"That's a lot of Vangs,"
said Buster.

"We even live on Vang Road,"
said Caitlyn.

CAITLYN

DIANE

ROSE

JOCEL

Dear Arthur,

Some girls here have a street named after them.

Do you think Elwood City would name a street after me?

Just wondering · · ·

Buster

Arthur Read
100 Main Street
Elwood

The Vangs were a clan of the Hmong people.

They had come to Wisconsin from Southeast Asia.

Dear Brain,

Do you know how to say "Hmong"?

(Hint: Pretend the "H" isn't there.)

Buster

The Vang girls were dancers.
They were getting ready for
a big tournament.

"Do you want
to watch us rehearse?"
they asked Buster.

"Sure!" he said.

the
VANG GIRLS'
DRESSING ROOM

ancine Frensky
Maple Drive Apt. 5
Elwood City

Later Buster visited the Vangs at home.

Ten of them
lived there together
with an uncle and a cousin.

Buster was amazed.

"I've only got my mom and dad,
and I don't even get them
at the same time."

Dear Binky,

My new friends have
a big garden
and a chicken coop.

In case you were wondering,
chickens are not
smarter than you think.

Buster

inky B
O Pin
Elwo

Mrs. Vang didn't know
how her daughters would do
in the dance tournament.

"If they do their very best
and feel good about it," she said,
"that's more important than winning."

For the contest,
the Vangs performed
the circle and
reverse circle fan dances.

Dear Francine,

A fan dance is fan-tastic.

You should try to see one someday.

Buster

Dear Muffy,

My friends the Vangs looked great performing i the dance festival.

You would like their costumes.

Buster

P.S. They didn't win but that's okay.

Muffy Crosswire
432 Valley View
Elwood

Buster said good-bye
to the Vangs
when the dance tournament
was over.

"I'll always think of you
when I see a fan,"
he said.

Dear Caitlyn,
Diane, Tiffany,
Jocelyn, Rose,
and Amanda,

After writing all your names,
I've run out of space.

Good luck with your dancing!

Buster